Delia Damson

Peter Potato

Belinda
Blackcurrant

Alice Apple

Polly
Pomegranate

Wee Willie
Water Melon

The Garden Gang
stories and pictures by

Jayne Fisher

Twelve year old **Jayne Fisher** is the youngest ever Ladybird author. She was only nine years old when she wrote these charming stories about fruit and vegetable characters.

Writing and drawing aren't Jayne's only interests. She has studied for the ribbon awards of the Royal School of Church Music, and plays the classical guitar and the recorder. Jayne sews, bakes, reads avidly, plays chess and keeps two gerbils and breeds stick insects.

But it is perhaps her own little garden at home which gave her the ideas for these stories. Jayne's bold, colourful felt-tipped pen illustrations are bound to appeal to young children and we can all learn a few lessons from the characters in the 'Garden Gang'.

Wee Willie
Water Melon

Ladybird Books Loughborough

Wee Willie Water Melon
lived in the beautiful
Highlands of Scotland.
He occupied a little
crofter's cottage
not far from the lochs,
set amongst the
sweet-scented heather.
As the smoke
curled from his
little chimney,
Wee Willie
looked on
with pride.

The joy of his life
was to wander
the Highlands
playing his bagpipes.
His music would float
over the hills
and streams,
and the only ones
to hear it
were the birds,
the bees and
the butterflies,
or any small animals
who happened to be
passing by.

One bright, sunny morning
as Wee Willie
was having his breakfast,
a letter plopped
through his letter box
onto the door mat.
It was from
his cousin,
Paul Pumpkin,
inviting him
for a holiday
down in the city.
Wee Willie was thrilled
because he had
never been to
a city before.

The following morning
Wee Willie Water Melon
packed a small suitcase,
and carrying
his precious bagpipes,
caught the little
number nine bus
which ran
once a day.
When he arrived
at the city
he could hardly
believe his eyes.

There were flats,
towering churches, shops,
factories with long,
smoking chimneys,
traffic which made
constant noise and
hundreds and
hundreds of people.
Cousin Paul Pumpkin
lived at the top
of a tall block of flats.
What a view!
Willie felt
he was back home
on the highest mountain,
with his head
in the clouds.

13

Paul gave Willie tea
because Willie was
tired and hungry
after his long journey,
and then Paul gave him
a piano recital.
All went well until
the following morning.
Willie couldn't go one day
without playing
his bagpipes,
and at 6 am
the practising began.
The neighbours
opened windows
to see who, or what
was making such a din.

14

15

But it wasn't
until this had happened
for several mornings
that they began
to complain.
Wee Willie Water Melon
was sad.
He couldn't enjoy life
without playing
his beloved bagpipes.
Paul just couldn't bear
to see Willie so sad.
Willie looked miserably
out of the window
with his bagpipes
there beside him
on the table.

So cousin Paul
gathered all
the neighbours together
in the hope
of solving the problem.
They came up with
the bright idea
of writing a letter
to the mayor
asking if their friend,
Wee Willie Water Melon,
could use the bandstand
in the city park
to practise his pipes,
when it was not in use
for band concerts.

They all waited anxiously
for a reply
from the Town Hall
and when at last
it arrived,
giving permission
for the bandstand
to be used,
Wee Willie
was overjoyed.
The very next morning,
as the birds started
their dawn chorus,
he set off
for the city park,
singing and skipping
as he went.

Being able to play
in the park bandstand
was not the only thing
that pleased Willie.
Because of
all his practising,
Willie had become
quite an expert
and this meant
that people
who wandered
into the park
stopped to hear him play.

Everybody now
enjoyed Willie's music.
They called and cheered
and he would stay
much later
at the bandstand
than he had ever intended
because of
the shouts of "more"
and all the clapping.
But the best thing
(or so Willie thought)
was that
whether in the city
or in his Highland home . . .

he
was
equally
happy!

Betty Beetroot

Betty Beetroot
suddenly found herself
without a home.
She arrived
in the garden of
the Garden Gang
quite by accident
one morning,
in a barrow
full of compost.

29

As the barrow
was tilted,
Betty felt herself
falling.
She rolled
along the ground
and hid beneath
a rhubarb leaf.
"Perhaps the gardener
won't see me here,"
she thought to herself.
When the barrow
was empty,
Mr Rake the gardener
went on his way.
Then Betty Beetroot
peered slowly round.

What a pleasant sight
met her eyes.
She was standing
in the most
beautiful garden
she had ever seen.
The sun was shining,
the birds were singing,
the bees were humming
and butterflies flitted
amongst the flowers.
The Garden Gang
were busy doing
their daily chores.
''I will surely find
a home here,''
she said.

33

She went to
Roger Radish
who was hiding, shyly,
behind a watering can.
"Do you know of
anywhere I could live?"
she asked.
Roger jumped into
the air at the sound
of her voice.
He frightened
a small bird
who was singing
on the can handle.
Roger quickly made
an excuse and dodged
behind a plant pot.

Betty looked round
and saw the Pea family
practising gymnastics.
''They look nice,''
she thought.
''I'll ask if
they can help.''
Percival Pea said,
she could have come
to his house,
but his grandchildren
were rather lively
and she might find it
crowded and noisy.
''Try the greenhouse,''
he said.

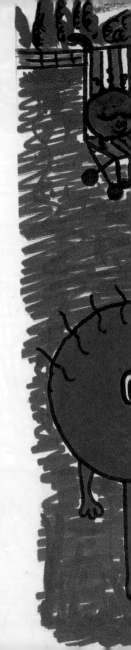

So Betty skipped
across the lawn
to the greenhouse.
Tim Tomato
was sitting
on a flowerpot
busily sketching
a feeding caterpillar.
He smiled at Betty
who was standing quietly
by the door.
Tim listened to her story
but then replied
that the greenhouse
was much too hot
for her.

Betty set off
up the path
and met Oliver Onion.
He was collecting pebbles
to make a rockery.
When she asked him
about a home,
he was so horrified
at the idea of
anyone else
cooking in his
precious kitchen,
that he immediately
said she would be better
living with Alice Apple,
Peter Potato or maybe
Gertrude Gooseberry.

First she met Alice Apple.
The dizzy heights
of the apple tree
made her feel giddy.
No, she could not
live there.
Peter Potato was
rather gruff and she felt
uneasy as she sat
in his parlour.
''I hope Gertrude
Gooseberry can help,''
she thought sadly.
She was now
tired and hungry,
but Gertrude was
no help either.

Poor Betty went back
to the compost heap
and sat on a stone
weeping.
"Whatever shall I do?"
she cried.
"Nobody wants me."
Suddenly,
Polly Pomegranate
danced daintily towards her.
Polly's lovely face
grew sad when
she saw Betty.
As Betty told her story,
Polly's face brightened.
She said, "Please come
and live with me."

Betty smiled
through her tears,
and hand in hand
they set off
across the garden
to Polly's house.
It was neat,
tidy and just right
for two people.
Polly showed Betty
her bedroom
and she was delighted.
The bed was comfortable
and the little chair
by the window
gave her a good view
of the beautiful garden.

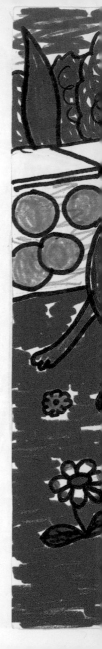

47

Betty gazed happily
round Polly's home.
"How lucky I am,"
she said.
"I will do all the
cleaning and cooking,"
Betty said,
"and you can
practise your ballet."
That night they ate
a delicious meal,
cooked by Betty,
and as they sat
in the firelight,
Betty felt happy
and safe with her
new found friend...

in
her
new
home!

Paul Pumpkin

Barnaby
Banana

Gertrude Gooseberry

Roger Radish